Dear Parent:
Your child's love of reading starts here!

Every child learns to read in a different way and at his or her own speed. Some go back and forth between reading levels and read favorite books again and again. Others read through each level in order. You can help your young reader improve and become more confident by encouraging his or her own interests and abilities. From books your child reads with you to the first books he or she reads alone, there are I Can Read Books for every stage of reading:

SHARED READING
Basic language, word repetition, and whimsical illustrations, ideal for sharing with your emergent reader

BEGINNING READING
Short sentences, familiar words, and simple concepts for children eager to read on their own

READING WITH HELP
Engaging stories, longer sentences, and language play for developing readers

READING ALONE
Complex plots, challenging vocabulary, and high-interest topics for the independent reader

I Can Read Books have introduced children to the joy of reading since 1957. Featuring award-winning authors and illustrators and a fabulous cast of beloved characters, I Can Read Books set the standard for beginning readers.

A lifetime of discovery begins with the magical words **"I Can Read!"**

Visit www.icanread.com for information
on enriching your child's reading experience.

I Can Read® and I Can Read Book® are trademarks of HarperCollins Publishers.

44 Cats: A Cat's Best Friend
Copyright © 2020 by Rainbow S.p.A. and Antoniano di Bologna. All rights reserved.
Printed in the United States of America.
44 Cats™ and all related logos, characters, and elements are trademarks of Rainbow S.p.A.
and Antoniano di Bologna. Series created by Iginio Straffi.
Nickelodeon is a trademark of Viacom International Inc.
No part of this book may be used or reproduced in any manner whatsoever without written permission except
in the case of brief quotations embodied in critical articles and reviews.
For information address HarperCollins Children's Books, a division of HarperCollins Publishers,
195 Broadway, New York, NY 10007.
www.icanread.com

Library of Congress Control Number: 2020934306   ISBN 978-0-06-300214-2

20 21 22 23 24 LSCC 10 9 8 7 6 5 4 3 2 1 ❖ First Edition

44 Cats™

A CAT'S
BEST FRIEND

Adapted by Megan Roth

HARPER

An Imprint of HarperCollinsPublishers

The cats are napping quietly
when they hear a dog barking.
"A dog?" Lampo asks.
"Inside Granny Pina's house?"

The cats get scared.

Dogs don't like cats

and cats don't like dogs.

The cats try to escape,

but then Granny walks in with the dog!

"Kitties, this is Terry the dog,"
Granny says.

"He wants to play."

She sets Terry down.

"Now you guys have fun!"

6

"Let's get out of here!"

Meatball says.

7

The cats run to the clubhouse.
But Terry runs after them.
"Don't you guys like to play?"
he asks.

8

"We love playing like cats."

Meatball says.

"Not like dogs!"

"Cats are like dogs," Terry says.

"We have four paws, fur, and a tail.

We eat treats.

We sit and we stay!"

"Cats are not like dogs," Milady says.

"No one tells a cat to sit or stay."

"That sounds nice," Terry says.

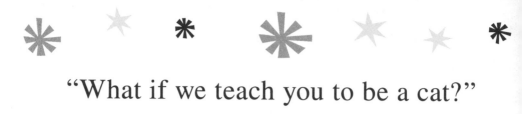

"What if we teach you to be a cat?"

Lampo asks.

"Yeah!" Terry cheers.

The cats teach Terry how to rub noses.

They even teach him how to meow.

13

"If you really want to be a cat,"
Milady says.

"You have to learn to climb trees."

 14

Terry takes a running start,
but slides right down the tree.

"I want to pass the tree test!"

Terry says.

"You can do it, Terry.

Believe in yourself," says Lampo.

Terry is ready to climb!

"I'm a cat.

I'm a cat.

I'm a cat."

Terry climbs the tree

and reaches the highest branch!

"Ta-da!" he says. "I'm a cat!"

"Now I'll jump off!" Terry says.

"No, it's too dangerous!" says Milady.

"Sit!

Stay!"

"No one tells cats what to do!"
Terry yells.

He slips and falls out of the tree.

And Terry lands on the other side

of the fence.

The cats look over the fence.

"Terry, are you okay?" Lampo asks.

Oh no! Trappy is on the other side!

Trappy is the neighbor's robotic dog.

Trappy does not like cats.

"Meow," Terry says.

Trappy thinks Terry is a cat.

The cats watch as the robot chases

Terry across the yard.

"We've got to help him!"

Pilou says.

The cats leap over the fence.

"Leave our friend alone!"

Lampo says to Trappy.

"More cats," says Trappy.

"I must attack!"

"No! We're dogs!" Pilou says.

"Woof-woof!"

"Cool!" Trappy says.

"Dog friends!"

With Trappy distracted,
the cats try to find Terry.
Instead of finding Terry,
they find Boss.
He controls Trappy.

"You may have fooled Trappy,"
Boss says.

"But I'll catch your friend!"

"Terry!" Lampo calls.

"Now would be a good time

to be a dog again!"

"A dog?" asks Terry.

"But will you still like me?"

"We will love you!" says Meatball.

Terry looks over at Boss. "Kitty!"

He licks Boss's face.

"Ew!" Boss says.

"Dog slobber!"

Then Terry jumps on Trappy
and starts licking his face too!

Terry's licks distract

Trappy and Boss.

The cats leap back over the fence.

They help Terry back over too!

"Thanks, buddy," Meatball says.

"I'm your buddy?" Terry asks.

"Of course!" the cats say.

"We're glad you're a dog."